## Books in the Linkers series

Homes discovered through Art & Technology
Homes discovered through Geography
Homes discovered through History
Homes discovered through Science

Toys discovered through Art & Technology
Toys discovered through Geography
Toys discovered through History
Toys discovered through Science

Myself discovered through Art & Technology
Myself discovered through Geography
Myself discovered through History
Myself discovered through Science

Water discovered through Art & Technology
Water discovered through Geography
Water discovered through History
Water discovered through Science

First paperback edition 1996
First published 1996 in hardback by A&C Black (Publishers) Limited
35 Bedford Row, London WC1R 4JH

ISBN 0-7136-4591-1
A CIP catalogue record for this book is available from the British Library.

Commissioned photographs by Zul Mukhida    Artwork by Malcolm Walker
Design by Jean Wheeler    Picture research by Liz Harman
**Consultant:** Philippa Webb

### Acknowledgements

Cephas; 10, 12, 19 (right), 23 (left), Chapel Studios; 16 (right), Bruce Coleman; Hans Reinhard 4 (left), Mark N
Boulton 4 (right), Peter A Hinchcliffe 7 (right) and cover, Patrick Clement 8 (left), 13 (left), John Shaw 23 (right),
James Davis; 3 (left), Eye Ubiquitious; 5, 7 (left), Edward Parker; 11 (right), 22, Positive Images; 3 (right), Tony Stone;
Dan Bosler 2, H Richard Johnstone 6, Warren Bolster 8 (right), Chris McCooey 11 (left), Zigy Kaluzny 16 (left), David
Woodfall 17, 21 (left), Pete Seaward 18, Richard During 19 (left), 20, Arnulf Husmo 21 (right), Zefa; 13 (right).

Printed and bound in Italy by L.E.G.O.

# Water

**discovered through**

## Geography

Karen Bryant-Mole

## Contents

**A & C Black • London**

# Water all around us

We see and use water every day of our lives.

**Homes**
Water is piped into our homes.
We use it for washing our bodies and our clothes.
We use it for drinking and cooking.
We use it for cleaning our homes
and our cars.

## Weather

There is water in our weather.
Water falls from the sky as rain.
On very cold days, the water freezes
and falls as snow or hail.

## Uses

Rivers, lakes and seas are full
of water.
We sail on it, swim in it, fish in it
and travel over it.
Can you think of
any other ways
in which we
use water?

# Ponds and lakes

A pond is a hollow or a dip in the ground that is filled with water.

## Natural ponds

The pond below is a natural pond. The ground dips down here and the hollow has filled up with rainwater. Wild plants grow around the pond. Small animals live in and around the pond.

## Artificial ponds

Some ponds are made by people. A hollow has to be dug and then lined with plastic, so that the water does not soak away.
If people want fish or plants for their pond, they have to buy them.

## Lakes

A lake is like a big pond. It is deeper than a pond and the water is usually colder. Most lakes are fed by rivers or streams. They have water flowing into them and out of them.

# Streams, rivers and waterfalls

Water always flows downhill.
The steeper the slope, the faster the water travels.

## Streams
Streams often begin high up in the hills. Sometimes the water comes up from below the ground.

Some streams are caused by melting snow or rainwater. As the stream runs downhill it is joined by other streams.

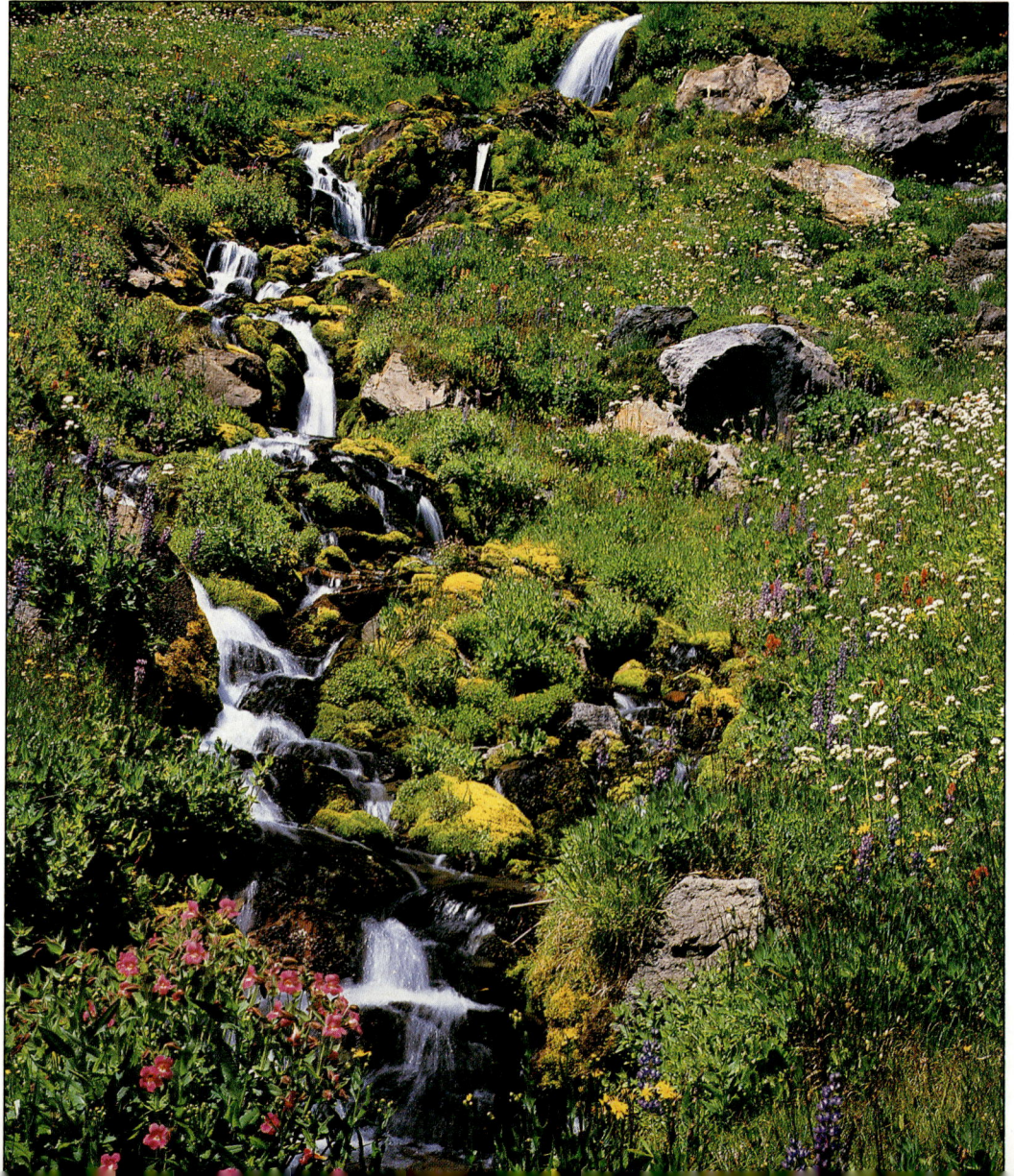

## Rivers

When a number of small streams have joined together, they become a river.
As the river flows along, it is joined by more streams and other, smaller, rivers.
These are known as tributaries.
Bridges and tunnels help us to cross rivers.

## Waterfalls

Sometimes the ground beneath a river or stream falls away very sharply.
When this happens, the water cascades from one level to the other as a waterfall.

# Seas and oceans

Seas and oceans surround the large areas of land on our planet, Earth.

**Estuaries**
All rivers eventually flow into the sea.
The end of the river is called the mouth of the river.
Sometimes the river mouth is so wide that the sea can flow in and out.
This is called an estuary.

## Salt
Seas and oceans are
huge areas of salty water.

In some parts of the world
the seas can be very calm.
In other parts they are
often extremely stormy.

## Earth
This is a globe.
It shows the lands, seas
and oceans of the world.
The seas and oceans are
coloured blue.
If you look at a globe,
you will see that more
of the Earth is covered
by water than by dry land.

# Reservoirs, dams and canals

Reservoirs, dams and canals have all been built by people.

## Reservoirs

Reservoirs are rather like large lakes.
We use reservoirs to collect and store water that can then be used in our homes.
Reservoirs are sometimes made by flooding an area of land with water.

## Dams

The reservoir below was made by building a huge wall, called a dam, across a river. The amount of water flowing through the dam is controlled by opening and closing pipes.

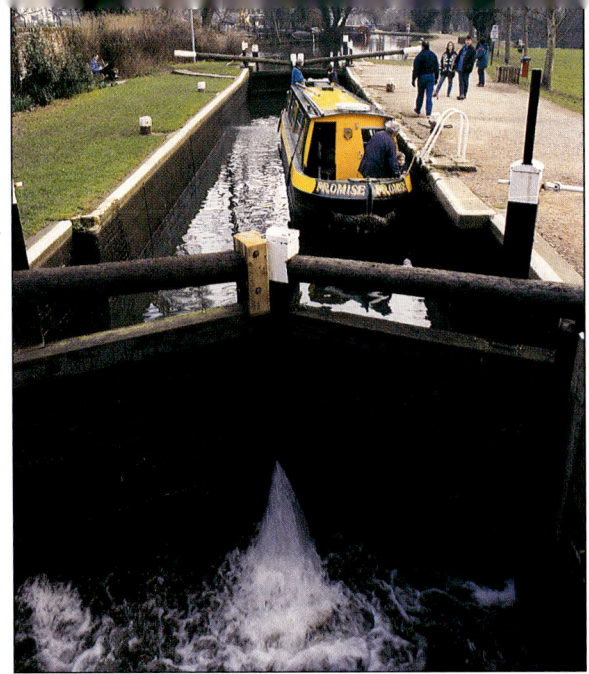

## Canals

Canals were built to be rather like roads for boats. They flowed where people wanted them to flow. Canals are flat. When a canal needs to go up or down a slope, it changes height in a series of steps, using special gates called lock gates.

# Harbours and ports

A harbour is an area of calm water that provides shelter for ships and boats.

**Harbours**
Some harbours are natural harbours, created by the shape of the land.

Many harbours have been built by people. They are usually built in sheltered places. Walls, called breakwaters, are built out into the sea to keep out the strong waves.

## Boats

Harbours are used by all sorts of boats.

The harbour in the picture on the right is used by passenger ships, sailing boats, fishing boats and huge ships that carry goods.

## Ports

Towns that are built around harbours are called ports.

The harbour provides jobs for the people who live in the town.

# Maps

Maps are drawings of places.
They often show water
as well as land.

**World**
This is a map of the world.
The seas and oceans are coloured blue.
The rest of the map shows land.

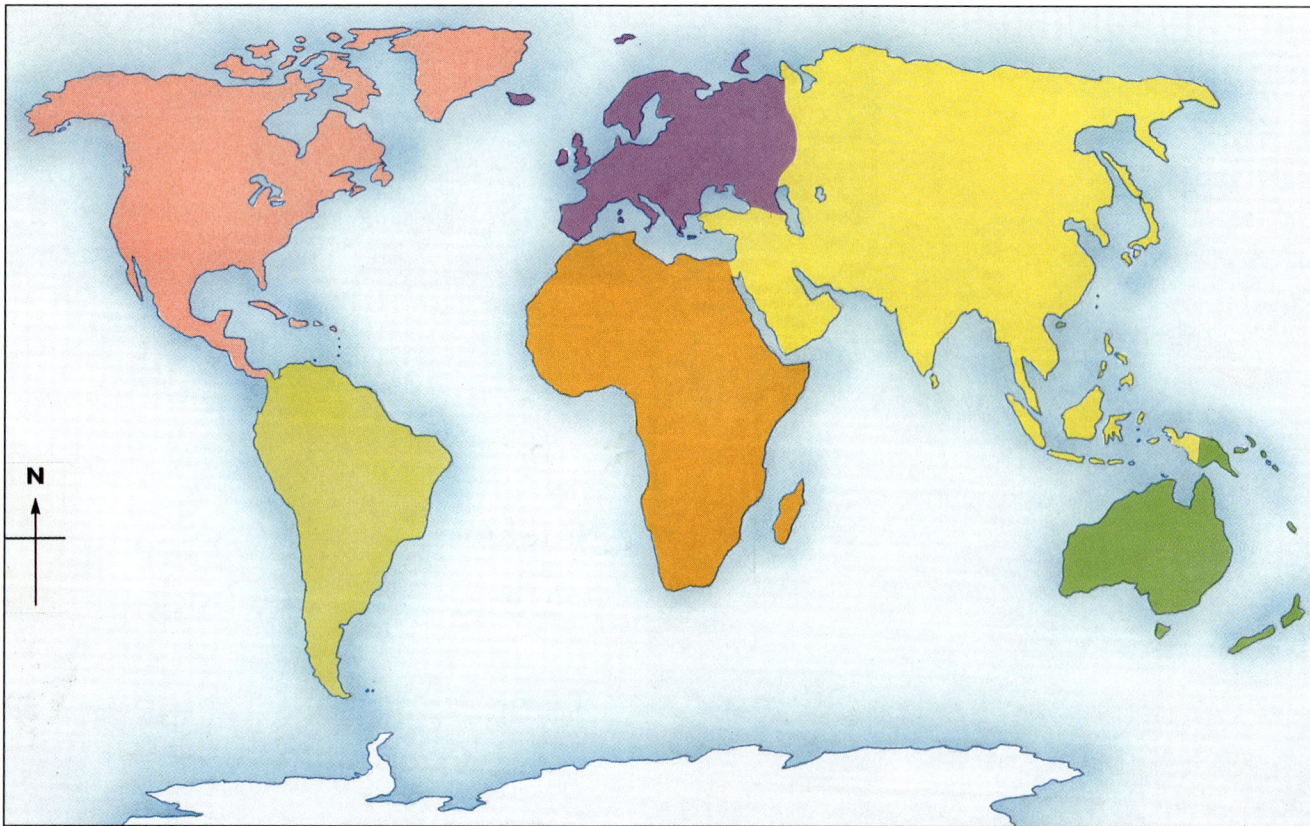

N

## River

This map shows a port and harbour.
The blue at the bottom is the sea.
There is a wide blue line leading
down to the sea.
This is a river.

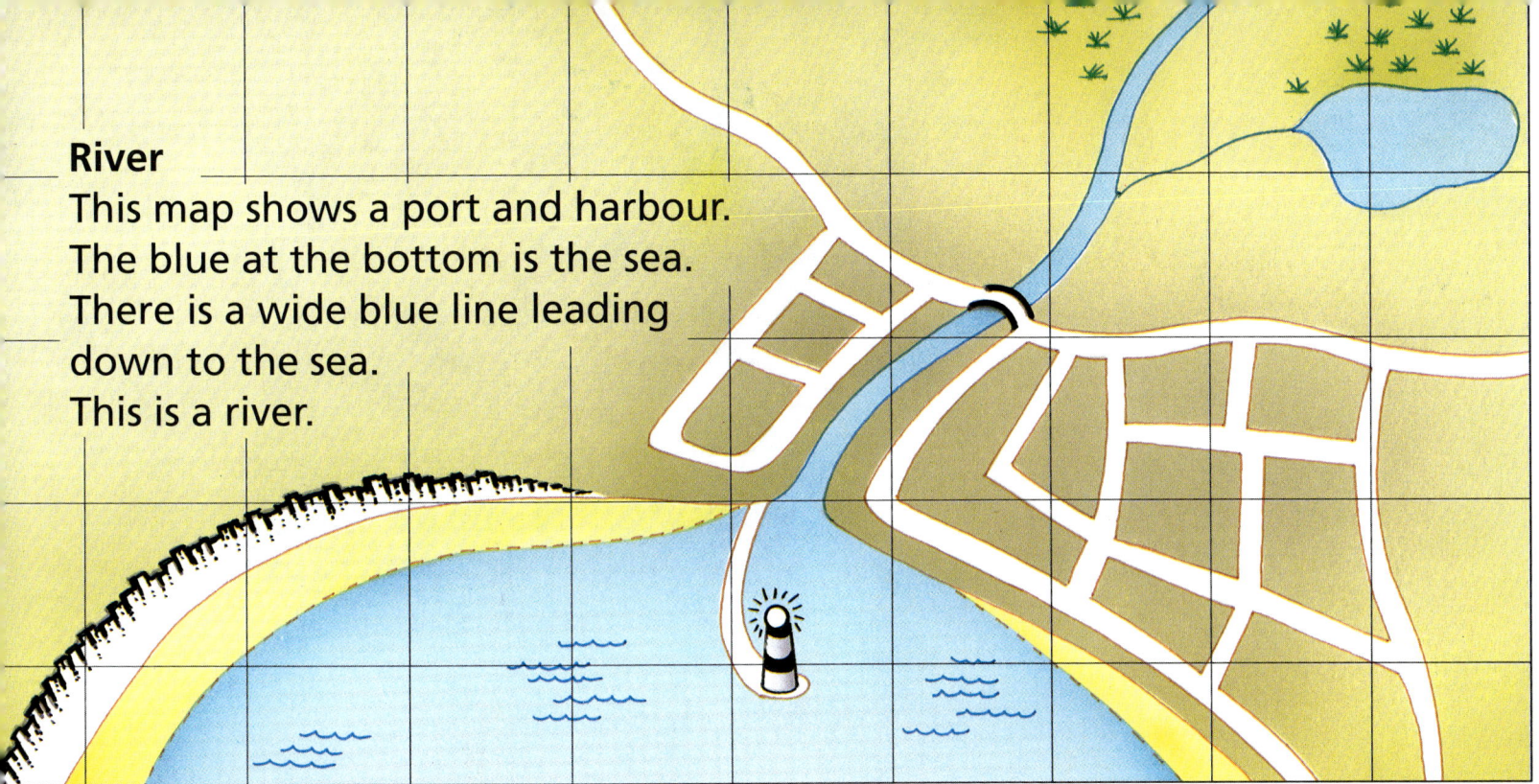

## Symbols

Most maps use signs, or symbols,
to tell you about the features
in the area.
Here are some symbols to do
with water.
If you look on a map you might be
able to see some symbols like these.

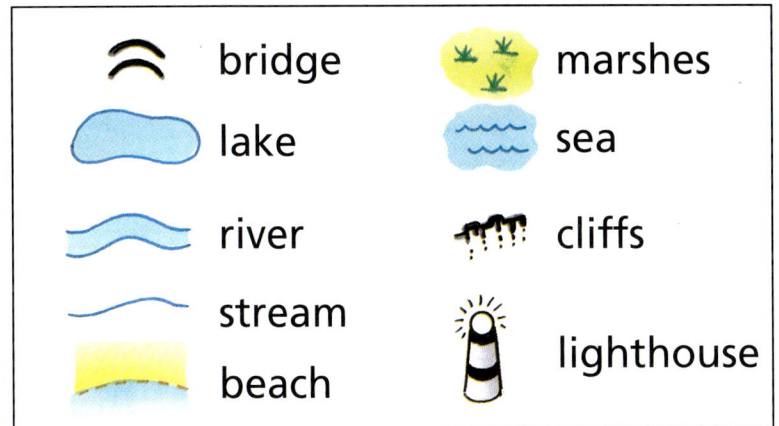

| | | | |
|---|---|---|---|
| bridge | | marshes | |
| lake | | sea | |
| river | | cliffs | |
| stream | | lighthouse | |
| beach | | | |

15

# Rain and floods

Water falls from clouds as rain.

## Farmers
Rain is very important to farmers.
All plants need water in order
to grow.
Rain has helped to produce the
wheat that is being cut in this field.

## Monsoons
Some countries of the world are
dry for many months and then wet
for many months.
The rains are brought in by strong
winds that are known as monsoons.
If the rains are late, the crops in these
countries may be ruined.

## Floods

If it rains very heavily, rivers can become dangerously full of water. The water in the river may overflow and flood the area all around. Floods often cause a lot of damage.

# Water travel

Boats and ships carry people and goods across water.

**Passenger boats**
Boats that carry people are called passenger boats.

Ferries are used to take people on short journeys over water. Huge boats, like this one, are called ocean liners. They take people across the world's seas and oceans.

## Cargo ships

Boats that carry goods,
rather than people,
are called cargo ships.
Many of these ships are
container ships.
The goods are packed
inside enormous
metal boxes.
The boxes can be loaded
neatly and easily.

## Water vehicles

There are many different ways
to travel across water.
This is a catamaran.
Yachts and hydrofoils are
water vehicles, too.

Can you think of any more?

# Fishing

Water is also a place where we find food.

**Nets**
This fishing boat goes out to sea for a few hours at a time.

The fishermen throw their nets overboard.
As the boat moves through the water, fish are caught in the net.

## Deep sea fishing

The fishing boat on the right travels far out to sea.

The fishermen are away for days at a time.

Some boats work in pairs.

Huge nets are slung between the two boats.

## Over-fishing

Many governments around the world are worried that too many fish are being caught.

Some fishermen are now only allowed to catch a certain amount of fish each week.

The holes in their nets must be big enough to let young fish escape.

# Pollution

Water sometimes becomes polluted, or dirty.

## Oil
The oil in this picture leaked into the sea, when an oil tanker hit a rock.
The orange oil boom is being used to try to stop the spread of the oil.

## Sewage

Every time we flush the toilet,
we produce waste called sewage.
Sewage is sometimes piped out to sea.
People are worried about sewage
polluting the water, making it unsafe
for swimming.
Seawater is now tested for pollution.

## Acid rain

Many factories produce gases that
are carried away in the air.
Some of these gases have been
known to pollute our rain causing
acid rain.
The trees in this picture have been
damaged by acid rain.

Water is too important to be taken
for granted. We must look after it.

# Glossary

**artificial**   not natural, made by people
**boom**   a floating tube or length of
   wood that stops things getting past
**cascades**   falls downwards quickly
**catamaran**   a boat with two main
   body sections
**created**   made

**crops**   food plants that are grown
   by farmers
**government**   the group of people
   chosen to run a country
**hydrofoil**   a boat that rises up out of
   the water on special fins, called foils
**shelter**   a safe place
**vehicle**   something that carries people
   or things from place to place

# Index

## How to use this book

Each book in this series takes a familiar topic or theme and focuses on one area of the curriculum: science, art and technology, geography or history. The books are intended as starting points, illustrating some of the many different angles from which a topic can be studied. They should act as springboards for further investigation, activity or information seeking.

The following list of books may prove useful.

## Further books to read

| Series | Title | Author | Publisher |
|---|---|---|---|
| Ask Isaac Asimov | What Causes Acid Rain? | Isaac Asimov | Heinemann |
| First Starts | Oceans | J. Palmer | Watts |
| Hand-Made Habitats | Pond | P. Wright | A&C Black |
| Jump! Ecology | Oceans | L. Baker | Watts |
| Lift Off! | Ships | J. Richardson | Watts |
| Links | Water | J. Baines | Wayland |
| Mapworlds | Water | Perham & Rowe | Watts |
| Picture Library | Rivers and Lakes | N. Barrett | Watts |
| Starting Ecology | Pond and Stream | C. Milkins | Wayland |
| Starting Geography | Water | Langthorne & Conroy | Wayland |
| Themes in Geography | Rivers | F. Martin | Heinemann |
| Tracks | Canals | Petty & Cash | A&C Black |
| Why do we have? | Rivers and Seas | C. Llewellyn | Heinemann |